On the Go with Pirate Pete and Pirate Joe

by A. E. Cannon

illustrated by Elwood H. Smith

PUFFIN BOOKS

For Pirate Geoffrey
—A.E.C.

For Maggie
—E.S.

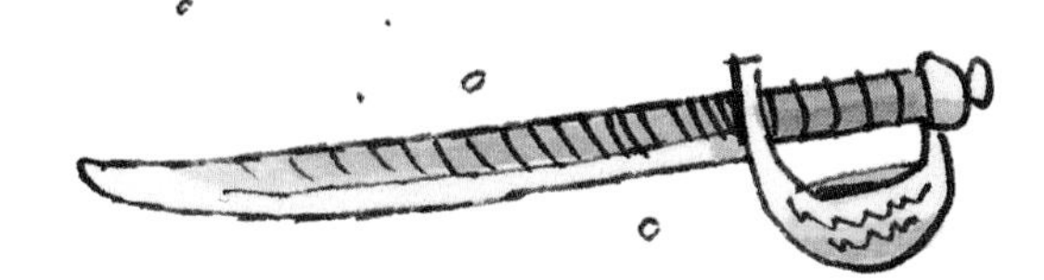

PUFFIN BOOKS
Published by the Penguin Group
Penguin Putnam Books for Young Readers, 345 Hudson Street,
New York, New York 10014, U.S.A.
Penguin Books Ltd, 80 Strand, London WC2R ORL, England
Penguin Books Australia Ltd, Ringwood, Victoria, Australia
Penguin Books Canada Ltd, 10 Alcorn Avenue, Toronto, Ontario, Canada M4V 3B2
Penguin Books (N.Z.) Ltd, 182-190 Wairau Road, Auckland 10, New Zealand

Penguin Books Ltd, Registered Offices: Harmondsworth, Middlesex, England

Published simultaneously in the United States of America by
Viking and Puffin Books,
divisions of Penguin Putnam Books for Young Readers, 2002

1 3 5 7 9 10 8 6 4 2

LIBRARY OF CONGRESS CATALOGING-IN-PUBLICATION DATA
Cannon, A. E. (Ann Edwards)
On the go with Pirate Pete and Pirate Joe / by Ann Cannon ;
illustrated by Elwood H. Smith.
p. cm.
Summary: Pirate Pete and Pirate Joe go out for seafood with their cat
Studley and their dog Dudley.
ISBN 0-670-03550-5 — ISBN 0-14-230136-1 (pbk.)
[1. Pirates—Fiction. 2. Humorous stories.] I. Smith, Elwood H., 1941-
ill. II. Title. PZ7.C17135 On 2002 [Fic]—dc21 2001005534

Printed in Hong Kong

Reading Level 1.8

Meet Pirate Pete and Pirate Joe!

This is Pirate Pete!

He is tall and thin.

This is Pirate Joe!

He is short and round.

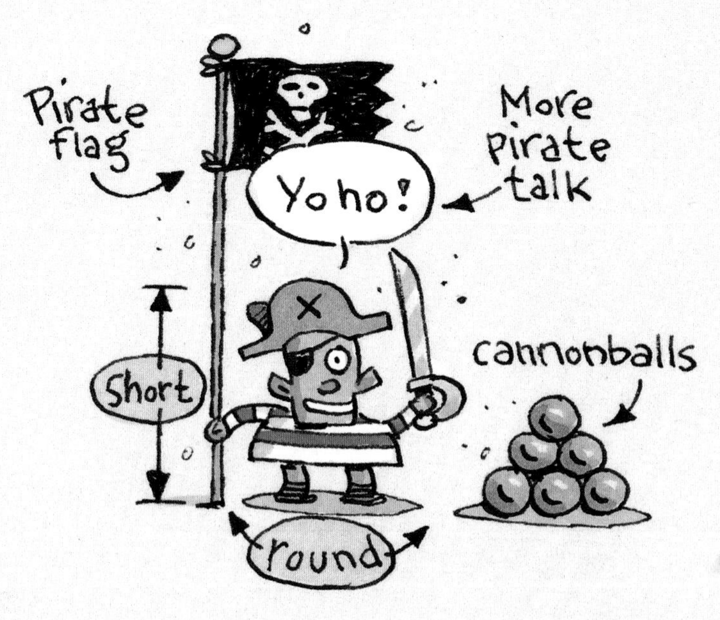

Pirate Pete and Pirate Joe live in a city by the sea. They live in a room they call the Crow's Nest.
They live with their dog (Dudley) and their cat (Studley).

Pirate Pete and Pirate Joe like to dance.

Pirate Pete does the hornpipe.

Pirate Joe likes to limbo.

They like to collect things.

Pirate Pete collects pirate hats.

Pirate Joe collects seashells.

Pirate Pete and Pirate Joe like to count their pirate coins.

Pirate Pete counts forwards.

Pirate Joe counts backwards.

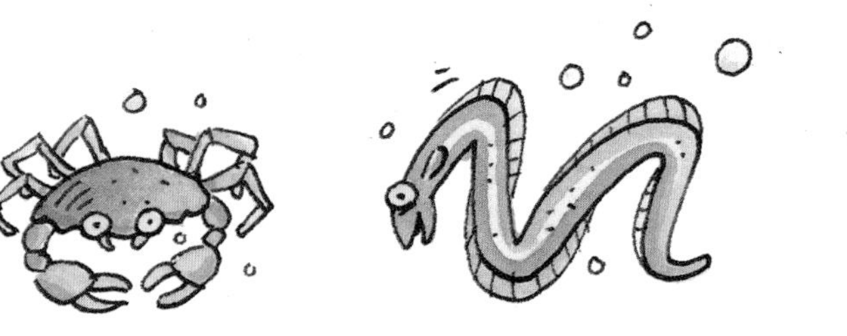

Both of them love to eat seafood.

Pirate Pete likes crabs.

Pirate Joe likes eels.

Every Sunday night the pirates

wash their patches.

They hang them out to dry.

Every Monday morning

their patches are dry.

These pirates are ready for action!

One Monday morning Pirate Pete asks,

"Are we pirates? Or are we pirates?"

"Aye! We are pirates!" says Pirate Joe.

"We are mean!" says Pirate Pete.

"We are not clean!" says Pirate Joe.

"We are not sweet!" says Pirate Pete.

"We have stinky feet!" says Pirate Joe.

"I am hungry for action!"

says Pirate Pete.

"I am hungry for seafood!"

says Pirate Joe.

"Argh! Let's steal something

good to eat!" says Pirate Pete.

"Aye aye, Skipper," says Pirate Joe.

The pirate pets are hungry, too.

They all sneak to the Crab Shack

across the street.

They hide inside the store room.

"Yum, yum!" say the pirates.

"Oh no! Here comes the cook!"

says Pirate Pete. "Duck!"

"Quack, quack," says Pirate Joe.

The cook comes.

The cook cooks.

The cook goes.

"Now!" says Pirate Pete.

"After you," says Pirate Joe.

"No, no. After you," says Pirate Pete.

The pirates look at each other.

"We are pirates who are not sweet,"

says Pirate Pete.

"We are pirates with stinky feet,"

says Pirate Joe.

"But we do not want to steal,"

says Pirate Pete.

His tummy grumbles.

"No. We only want to eat,"

says Pirate Joe.

His tummy rumbles.

The pirates are sad.

What can they do?

"I know!" says Pirate Pete. "Let's buy

seafood with our pirate coins!"

Pirate Pete counts his coins forwards.

Pirate Joe counts his coins backwards.

"Yoo-hoo, Cook!" says Pirate Joe.

"Ahoy, boys!" says the cook.

"Here is some seafood for you!"

Pirate Pete does the hornpipe.

Pirate Joe does the limbo.

Dudley barks and Studley purrs.

Yo ho ho!

And away they go!

Pirate Joe and Pirate Pete Look for a Ship

"Yo ho!" says Pirate Pete.

"Yo ho!" says Pirate Joe.

"Are we pirates? Or are we pirates?"

asks Pirate Pete.

"Aye! We are pirates!" says Pirate Joe.

"Then where is our ship?"

asks Pirate Pete.

Pirate Joe looks around.

"Is it in the shop?"

"No!" says Pirate Pete.

"We do not have a ship in the shop!

We do not have a ship!

We have never had a ship!"

"Oh no!" says Pirate Joe.

"We are pirates," says Pirate Pete,

"without a ship!"

"Boo hoo!" says Pirate Joe.

"We need a ship!" says Pirate Pete.

"Aye aye, Skipper!" says Pirate Joe.

"We need a ship! We want to look like pirates!" says Pirate Pete.

"Aye!" says Pirate Joe.

"We need a ship! We want to *be* pirates!" says Pirate Pete.

"Yo ho ho and a bottle of pop!" says Pirate Joe.

"We need to buy a ship today!" says Pirate Pete.

"Let's go!" says Pirate Joe.

Pirate Pete and Pirate Joe walk to the seashore.

They talk as they walk.

They walk as they talk.

“Pirates name their ships,”

says Pirate Pete.

“Is that so?” asks Pirate Joe.

“We will need to name our new ship,”

says Pirate Pete.

“What will we name our new ship?”

asks Pirate Joe. “Bill? Bob? George?”

“No! We will name our new ship the

Jolly Roger!” says Pirate Pete.

“Yo ho!” says Pirate Joe.

Pirate Pete and Pirate Joe see a ship
at the seashore.
It is big. It is black. It is for sale!
"We want to buy your big black ship,"
says Pirate Pete to the captain.
"Aye aye, maties!" says the captain.
"All aboard!"
"After you, Pirate Joe,"
says Pirate Pete.
"No, no. After you, Pirate Pete,"
says Pirate Joe.
"You go first," says Pirate Pete.
"You go first," says Pirate Joe.
"No!" says Pirate Pete.
"No!" says Pirate Joe.

Ahoy!
Argh!
Pirate ship for sale

"Are you afraid of the water?"

asks Pirate Pete.

"Yes," says Pirate Joe.

"I am afraid of the water.

It is deep. It is dark.

It is full of sharks who crunch and

sharks who munch."

"I am afraid of the water, too,"

says Pirate Pete.

"I am afraid of sharks who munch and

sharks who crunch."

"We cannot buy your ship,"

says Pirate Pete to the captain.

Pirate Pete and Pirate Joe are very sad.

"Would you like to buy my van?"

asks the captain.

"It is big. It is black.

It has a pirate flag. It says

PIRATES 'R' US on the front.

It is called the *Jolly Roger*."

Pirate Pete looks at Pirate Joe.

Pirate Joe looks at Pirate Pete.

"Sold!" say the pirates.

Pirate Pete does the hornpipe.

Pirate Joe does the limbo.

Yo ho ho!

And away they go!

Pirate Pete and Pirate Joe Find a Parrot

"Yo ho!" says Pirate Pete.

"Yo ho!" says Pirate Joe.

"We have a ship now,"

says Pirate Pete.

"But something is still

missing from our pirate lives!"

"Pirate girls!" says Pirate Joe.

"No!" says Pirate Pete. "Pirate parrots!"

"Oh!" says Pirate Joe.

"Let's find a parrot for ourselves,"

says Pirate Pete.

"Let's go!" says Pirate Joe.

Pirate Pete and Pirate Joe get in
their big black van.
They drive the *Jolly Roger*
to the pet store.

"Take us to your parrots,"

says Pirate Pete.

"We have three good parrots

for sale today," says the woman

who works at the store.

"Walk this way."

The first parrot is big and red.

"This parrot sings opera,"

says the woman.

Pirate Pete and Pirate Joe

shake their heads *no.*

"That is not good enough for us!"

Next
Show:
3:00

The second parrot is big and white.

"This parrot speaks three languages—

English, French, and Pig Latin,"

says the woman.

Pirate Pete and Pirate Joe

shake their heads *no.*

"That is not good enough for us!"

The third parrot is big and blue.

"This parrot is the best parrot of all.

He can read a book while hanging

upside down."

Pirate Pete and Pirate Joe

shake their heads *no*.

"That is not good enough for us!"

"You do not like the red parrot that

sings, the white parrot that talks, or

the blue parrot that reads,"

says the woman. "I cannot help you."

"What about that bird?"

asks Pirate Pete.

Pirate Pete points to a parrot.

He is small. He is gray.

He is wearing a patch.

“That is Bucko,” says the woman.

“You do not want Bucko. He is bad

news. He thinks he is a pirate.

And he can only say one thing.”

Pirate Pete does the hornpipe.

Pirate Joe does the limbo.

“*That is good enough for us!*” they say.

The pirates take Bucko

to the *Jolly Roger*.

"I wonder what he says,"

says Pirate Joe.

"Yo ho!" says Bucko.

"Yo ho! Yo ho! Yo ho!"

And away they go!